THE GOOSE THAT WAS A WATCHDOG

THE GOOSE THAT WAS A WATCHDOG

by Wilma Pitchford Hays

Illustrated by Nelson McClary

Little, Brown and Company   Boston   Toronto

By *Wilma Pitchford Hays*
Illustrated by Wesley Dennis

THE LITTLE HORSE THAT RACED A TRAIN
LITTLE LONE COYOTE
THE PUP WHO BECAME A POLICE DOG
LITTLE HAWAIIAN HORSE
LITTLE HURRICANE HAPPY

Illustrated by Nelson McClary

THE GOOSE THAT WAS A WATCHDOG

Weekly Reader Children's Book Club Edition

For my grandson,
STEPHEN

TAD VOGEL stepped off the school bus at the lane that led to Oak Grove Farm and saw a big delivery truck beside a cotton field. The geese had come. He had hoped and wished that something would keep them away. Their coming meant that his family would have to move from the farm which had always been their home.

"Where am I going to find work?" Tad's father had said at supper when he first heard that Mr. Collins was going to buy geese to weed the cotton fields. "I don't know anything but cotton."

His father had turned his rough black hands. "That's all I've ever done. Plant cotton, chop weeds with a hoe. Pick and haul cotton to the gin."

"Don't fret," Tad's mother had said. "Tad, take baby Lou on the porch while I clear the dishes."

Tad carried his baby sister to the porch rocking chair. While he sang her to sleep, he could hear his father and mother talking.

His mother believed that things would come out right if you did your best. Yet half the other share-croppers had moved from the farm a year ago, when Mr. Collins began to pick cotton with machines instead of by hand. Now geese would weed out the grass better and cheaper than field hands could. What was a man like his father to do?

Tad ran up the lane between fields where rows of spring-green cotton plants were breaking through

the ground. He stopped beside the delivery truck
and called to the red-haired driver.

"Maybe the geese will eat the tender cotton," he
said hopefully. "They won't last long on this farm
if they do that."

The driver laughed. "Geese would starve before they'd eat cotton plants," he said.

"Why?" Tad asked.

The driver shook his head. "I don't know *why*," he said. "Geese just don't eat cotton. But they sure like Johnson grass. Looks like there's plenty sprouting here, too."

Tad looked at the acres of cotton along the river. Last year the wide Mississippi, rolling down to Memphis, had flooded. Muddy water overflowed and carried weed and grass seed far into the carefully tended fields. The weeder-geese would have to work fast if there was to be a cotton crop this year.

Two men were lifting crates from the truck. Tad looked through the wire mesh covers on the crates, and he could scarcely believe his eyes.

These were not geese. The crates held goslings, hundreds of downy baby geese not much larger than Tad's fist. They stood on little pancake feet as yellow as their slender bills.

"Babies like these work the fields?" Tad cried.

The men grinned. "You just turn them loose in the cotton and see," one man said. "Of course you have to protect them to keep dogs or fox from eating them. But give them a little shade and plenty of water. They'll take care of the grass all right."

The goslings were opening their mouths as if they were thirsty now. Tad ran to a drainage ditch nearby and brought back water in his cupped hands. He sprinkled their unlifted open throats. The goslings gave thankful beeps and climbed on top of each other trying to get nearer to him.

Tad ran for more water. He returned to find Mr. Collins looking at the goslings.

The farm owner pushed back his wide-brimmed hat. He seemed as surprised as Tad to find the goslings so young.

"They're going to take some looking after," Mr. Collins said.

"Yes, sir," Tad said and sprinkled water to the goslings.

Mr. Collins watched him and seemed to be thinking. "Tad," he said, "the superintendent of the

hatchery tells me that one man and a boy can look
after all the goslings for this farm. How would you
like to be the boy?"

"I would," Tad said. "I sure would."

Mr. Collins smiled. "I've asked your father to take charge of the geese," he said. "A man from the hatchery will explain what is to be done. Then your father and you will be responsible for their care until fall."

Tad ran past Oak Grove where Mr. Collins lived in the big house, past the chicken house where the rooster crowed at him, and into the weathered gray house where his mother was cooking grits and ham for supper.

"We don't have to move," he cried. "We're going to stay right here and take care of the weeder-geese."

His mother gave him a cake bowl she had saved for him to scrape. "I told you not to fret," she said. "When changes come, they're just as likely to be good as bad."

Each day as soon as he came from school, Tad helped his father. They built low fences around the cotton fields.

"Geese aren't high flyers," his father told him, as

10

he drove stakes into the ground. Tad tacked on the poultry netting.

They hauled empty cotton-picking trailers to the end of the fields nearest their house. Here the geese slept on clean straw under the trailers.

12

Tad and his father built water troughs at the
other end of the fields. The little geese ate their
way through the fields to the water each morning.
They ate their way back to their shelters every
night.

Tad saw that one little goose was always out ahead of the others. He watched her coming between rows on her little flat feet. She dipped her slender neck this way, then that. With her strong bill she dug down and ripped up grass roots without disturbing a single cotton plant.

"That little goose eats anything as long as it's grass," Tad said to his father. "Johnson grass, Ber-

muda grass, crabgrass, foxtail. It's all the same to her."

And between grass ripping, she talked to herself in wispy soft goose language that sounded as if she were happy.

"Come on Em," Tad called to her each evening.

He didn't know whether the little gray goose was a boy or a girl, but he named her Emmy. She acted like a girl, he thought.

She was so pleased when he sprayed her with the hose from the water wagon. After her shower bath, Em settled down on the straw under the trailer and preened her growing gray and white feathers with her bill. When she had combed every fluffy feather into place, she tucked her head under her wing and went to sleep.

Night was the time when Tad and his father had to watch most carefully. The shelters were near the house so they could hear the geese gabble if a dog or fox tried to steal a goose dinner.

One night after school was out for the summer and the geese had grown to a good size, Tad was waked by a great gabbling and honking. He pulled on his jeans and raced to the shelter. His father was right behind him.

In the moonlight the geese rushed to meet them, circling and pushing against their legs. Tad's father swung a flashlight around, beamed toward the ground.

"I don't see dog or fox tracks," he shouted above the gabbling din.

Em made a long skimming run to reach Tad. Her long neck was arched and her wings spread wide. Tad knelt and touched her back. She placed her slick yellow bill to his ear and whispered her fears.

"Em sure wants to tell me what it was," Tad said. "Maybe a skunk. I saw one yesterday."

"A human skunk," his father said and pointed his flashlight to show the print of a big shoe heel on the ground. "Maybe he thought geese are as easy to steal as chickens, but he knows better now."

Tad was thankful that geese had their own alarm horns. Their honks made them the noisiest creatures on the farm when they were excited. They began to calm down now. He gave Em a final pat and stood up.

She followed him to the gate. He tried to push her back with his foot when he opened it. She slipped past him and padded along behind him to the house, whispering and hissing at the dark.

Tad caught her and started back to the shelter. She was quite an armload now. She arched her long neck and buried her bill in Tad's thicket of black hair. In soft whispering goose language she tried to tell Tad that she wanted to stay with him.

"Why not?" Tad said to her.

Em was not housebroken. His mother wouldn't welcome her inside. But there was a flower box on the windowsill outside his bedroom. The petunias

were straggly and dried from the summer heat anyway. Tad put Em on the window box with only
the screen between the little goose and his bed.

She settled herself, making little beeps, "Quonk,
quonk," to ask if Tad was there.

From his bed, Tad put his nose against the screen
and quabbled back at her. She liked that and they
kept up the conversation until Tad fell asleep.

After that Em would not sleep anywhere else.
Each morning she fluttered to the ground and Tad
took her to work. But when she was not weeding
cotton, Em followed Tad around.

She thought she owned the place. She quonked
at every stranger who came into the yard — dog, pig
or person. She ran out her long neck tipped with
her strong hard bill. With wings spread wide, she
dashed at every intruder, honking, "Quonk, quonk."
She seemed to be asking, "Have you a right to be
here?"

And if they did not have a right, they ran.

"Em's a real watchdog," Tad said to his mother.
"She sure guards baby Lou. Did you see her?"

His mother nodded, smiling.

When Lou began to crawl, her father had tacked
poultry netting around four porch posts to keep her
safe. Em squatted down beside the baby's pen and
talked to her in soft wispy sounds. She brought

clumps of Johnson grass, roots and all, and dropped her presents in the baby's lap.

Little Lou leaned over too far and bumped her head and cried.

Em raced to the front door, jawing for someone to come and see what was the matter with her baby!

Tad picked up his little sister. She wasn't hurt.

His mother laughed and shook her head. "Nothing's going to harm this family," she said, "long as that goose watchdog is here to honk the alarm."

The gray goose was so much fun that the summer seemed to skim by. One morning Tad realized that the cotton was grown. The geese were, too. He had better get in all the fishing he could before he had to start back to school.

He whistled as he cut through the cotton field, fish pole over his shoulder. He knew where catfish lived in a creek that emptied into the river.

When Tad reached the fence beside the road, he found that Em was following him. She tilted her head and called in her softest voice, "Quonk? Quonk?"

Tad grinned. That little goose was begging,
"Take me with you, please take me."

Tad lifted her over the fence and she padded up

the road beside him. "Quonk, quonk," she honked loud and happy now that she had her way.

Then Em discovered the white traffic line in the middle of the road. She stretched her neck and lowered her bill above the line, and marched up it as if it had been painted just for her.

Tad laughed until a car horn sounded behind

them. He stepped to the side of the road and called to Em. She kept right on walking the white line, fascinated.

The car stopped. Tad ran and rescued Em. Then he saw the man in the car was Mr. Collins.

"Is that the goose watchdog I've been hearing about?" he asked.

"Yes," Tad said, then added hastily, "but Em's a good weeder, too. She only follows me evenings — and sometimes on a holiday."

Mr. Collins laughed. He knew that geese ate weed-grass seven days a week and didn't know what a holiday was.

"The cotton weeding is over for this year anyway," he said. "I've got a buyer coming for the geese tomorrow or the next day."

"A buyer?" Tad said. He could not believe that Mr. Collins was going to sell the geese. "Won't we need them next year?"

"Don't worry, I'll buy goslings again in the spring," Mr. Collins said. "No use feeding geese through the winter with nothing for them to do."

Tad watched Mr. Collins drive away. He didn't
feel like going fishing now. But Em saw the creek
and padded across the grass gabbling about a swim.

Tad sat on the creek bank and held his pole. He
watched Em dip her head and lift water in her
bill and send it running down her back. She dived
and ruffled her feathers. When she finished her
swim, she ran along the bank catching bugs, as
happy as she could be.

He just couldn't let a buyer take Em away.

He caught five catfish and took them home to his mother, and she fried them for supper.

At the table his father said to him, "Sure are good catfish. Why aren't you eating yours?"

"Mr. Collins is going to sell the geese," Tad said. "Maybe tomorrow."

"I know," his father said. "They'll bring a good price now."

"How much for one goose?" Tad asked. He had saved sixty cents this summer. Maybe he could buy Em.

"I don't know rightly," his father said. "A gosling costs about three dollars. A grown goose ought to bring two or three times that much."

Tad choked and it wasn't on a catfish bone. He had never in his life had that much money at one time. And his father and mother could not spare money for something they did not need.

His mother handed him a cookie as if she knew how he felt. His father changed the subject.

"We had a letter today," he said. "The big school

in town is finished. All fifth graders out this way are going to the new school this year."

Tad looked at his father and mother. They must know how he hated to change schools. "This sure isn't my day," he said.

"You got to get a good education," his father said. "Know more than how to raise cotton."

"Maybe you'll like it," his mother said. "It's a

beautiful school. You'll ride the same bus — just go on into town."

Tad laid down his fork. He couldn't eat another bite. When he went to town with his family, he had passed the big school as it was being built. The halls looked about a mile long with rooms and rooms and rooms. He'd feel lost in a place like that. With strange kids and strange teachers, too.

"If I have to go to school at all," Tad said, "I want to stay where I know everyone."

"You don't start until Monday," his mother said. "By that time, you may change your mind."

Tad was still miserable when he went to bed. Em gabbled softly through the screen. She had very keen hearing and tried to tell him what she heard each night. Tonight she kept turning her head from side to side, inspecting the dark as if there was something out there too horrible to describe.

Finally she ran her bill across the screen, then dipped her head, waiting. Tad knew she wanted him to gabble back at her. He could not.

Tomorrow or the next day the buyers would

come. Em would be gone. If that wasn't enough, on Monday he had to go to a strange new school in the town, and he was scared.

Finally he went to sleep and thought he heard a chicken squalk. Something was after his mother's chickens. He tried to get up but he could not move no matter how hard he tried.

Em's muttering waked Tad. He drew a big breath of relief. He had only been dreaming. There was nothing wrong.

Em didn't seem to agree with him. She leaned against the screen, her long neck arched. She was listening and hearing something he could not hear.

Tad touched the screen. Em let out one frightened "Quonk," fluttered from the window box and was silent.

Tad tried to see her through the screen but could not. He slipped out of the house so he would not wake anyone. There was no moon but the stars were bright, and he could see a little.

Em was not under the window box. He ran around the house. She was not there.

Could she have gone for a drink of water? Em was always thirsty when she was excited.

He hurried toward the water tank near the chicken house at the edge of Oak Grove. He stubbed his bare foot and cried, "Ouch."

He stood on one foot, holding his aching toe. Without a sound Em came up behind him. She leaned against his leg and hissed into the darkness, a hiss only Tad could hear.

She was saying, "They're after us."

Tad forgot his aching toe and listened with Em.

Was that wind rustling the trees? No, there wasn't any wind. But there was a sound under the trees like feet walking on fallen leaves. Shuffling feet. The way men move their feet when they are carrying something heavy.

A chicken squalked. All at once Tad knew. Even in his sleep, he really had heard a chicken squalk before. Someone *was* stealing his mother's chickens.

Then he saw the dark sides of a truck almost hidden under the overhanging branches of an oak tree. This was no field hand taking a chicken dinner. These were thieves stealing the whole flock that his family depended upon for eggs and meat.

He turned to run and get his father, but right beside him were two men. They grabbed Tad's shoulder.

"What we going to do with him until we get away?" one man asked.

All Tad could see of them was the whites of their eyes and teeth. He was too scared to yell.

"Lock him in the chicken house," the other man said.

Tad yelled then, but he was sure his voice did not carry all the way to the house. Mr. Collins's house was just as far away on the other side of Oak Grove. No one would hear him.

But he had forgotten Em. When the men started pushing Tad toward the chicken house, Em gave a great angry "Quonk, quonk." She flew at the thieves with wings outstretched, quonking and gabbling.

The men kicked at her and threw up their arms to protect their faces. Tad jerked away.

"That goose'll wake everyone for miles," one thief said. They ran toward the truck.

Em had waked the geese sleeping under the cotton trailers. They joined in a chorus of honking that no one could sleep through.

Lights went on in Tad's house. Lights went on in Mr. Collins's house. Lights went on in the houses of field hands all along the road.

The thieves got the truck started and whizzed away. A shotgun went off down the lane, but the truck got by. Another shotgun fired. There was a bang as if a tire blew. A crash as if the truck went off the road and hit something.

Tad caught Em up in his arms and ran toward the road. By the time he got there, a half dozen men with flashlights had tied the hands of the thieves behind them, and were leading them to a car. His father and Mr. Collins were looking into the back of the truck at the cackling hens.

"They have all my chickens, too," Mr. Collins said. "Looks like they'd have got away with every chicken on the place if it hadn't been for Tad."

He turned and smiled.

Tad said, "Not me. Em saved the chickens. She's a real watchdog."

Mr. Collins looked at Tad holding Em with both arms, she was so heavy. She buried her bill gently in Tad's hair.

"She is a fine watchdog, at that," Mr. Collins said. "The thieves must have fed my dogs something to put them to sleep tonight."

"We need Em here, don't you think?" Tad asked. "She doesn't eat much but grass and water. I'd take care of her."

"Well," Mr. Collins said. "She earned her keep

with this night's work. So did you, Tad. You can have her."

"To keep?" Tad said. "For my own?"

"To keep."

Tad grinned his thanks.

"You better get back to the house," his father said. "Your mother will be upset until she knows you are all right."

Tad took Em home and saw his mother standing in the lighted doorway. "I'm coming," he called, "soon as I put Em to bed."

He put the goose on the window box and she began her settling-down-for-the-night conversation. She ran her bill close to Tad's ear and gabbled softly, "Quonk, quonk."

She seemed to be saying, "You were miserable tonight and would not talk to me. But it's all right now."

Things had come out all right about the geese, Tad thought. A few months ago he had hoped and wished the weeder-geese would not come. Now he wouldn't trade his gray goose for any pet anywhere.

But he still had to go to the strange school on Monday.

Maybe that change would turn out right, too. The new school might not be so bad when he got used to the many rooms, strange kids, and strange teachers. Em had proved that a change was just as likely to be good as bad.

"Quonk, quonk," she whispered as if she agreed with him.

This time Tad gabbled right back at her.